THIS

BOOK

BELONGS

TO _____

DISNEY'S
SMALL WORLD LIBRARY
A VERY SPECIAL NEW YEAR
An Adventure in India

GROLIER ENTERPRISES INC.

DANBURY, CONNECTICUT

© The Walt Disney Company. All rights reserved.
Printed in the United States of America.
Developed by The Walt Disney Company in conjunction with Nancy Hall, Inc.
ISBN: 0-7172-8221-X

"We're almost there," said Morty to Ferdie, studying his map. They were on their way to visit their pen pal, Chanda, who lived in a tiny village in southern India.

Chanda had been waiting impatiently by her window all morning. She rushed to meet Morty and Ferdie as soon as they walked through the gate.

"Welcome!" she cried. "I am so glad you're here! Where is your Uncle Mickey? I thought he was coming with you."

"He'll be here in two days," replied Ferdie.

"Good!" exclaimed Chanda. "Then he will be here in time to join us for Divali, the Festival of Lights. That's when we celebrate the New Year."

Chanda led the way into her house, where her parents had dinner waiting. Morty and Ferdie tasted many new foods. Morty's favorite was a lentil dish. Ferdie loved a mixture of vegetables and spices that they ate with a special kind of bread.

As they were finishing their meal, Chanda said, "The next few days are going to be very busy around here."

"Yes, indeed," declared Chanda's father. "There is so much to do to prepare for Divali."

"Everything must be very clean," explained Chanda's mother, "or Lakshmi, who brings good luck and prosperity, will not visit our home this year."

"We can help," offered Morty and Ferdie.

The next morning, everyone got up early. Morty and Ferdie helped Chanda scrub the kitchen pots until they gleamed like new. Next they helped Chanda's father whitewash the whole house, inside and out.

After they rested and ate lunch, Chanda took her guests for a tour of her village. She showed them her school and a busy outdoor market.

As they approached the village well, they heard a loud shriek.

"Oh, no!" a woman yelled. "Can't you ever watch where you put those big feet of yours?"

"Uh-oh!" said Chanda. "It sounds like Ram is in trouble again. Let's hurry!"

Around the corner they came face-to-face with a little elephant drinking from a puddle. A row of overturned water jugs lay at his feet. The elephant lumbered over to Chanda as soon as he saw her.

"This is Ram," she said. "His mother died when he was a baby. Our village has adopted him."

Ram nuzzled Chanda's cheek with his trunk. Chanda hugged him back.

"He may be a little clumsy," said Chanda, smiling, "but he's a lot of fun!"

That evening, Morty and Ferdie helped Chanda and her family make boxes out of colored paper. On Divali, Chanda's mother and grandmother would fill the boxes with the delicious candies they had been making all week. Morty's mouth watered as he stared at the big bowl of candy on the kitchen table. Each piece was shaped like a different animal or flower.

"Would you like to taste one?" asked Chanda's mother. "We must be certain that they are good enough to serve to company."

"These are great!" said Morty. "In fact, I think they taste too good to give away!"

Later, before they fell asleep, Chanda told Morty and Ferdie about her favorite Divali custom.

"Tomorrow evening," she whispered, "everyone will place golden oil lamps on their roofs and windowsills, so that Lakshmi will be able to find her way to every home."

"Will we be able to see her?" Morty whispered back.

"No," replied Chanda. "She visits only when everyone is sound asleep. But just wait until you see how beautiful the village will look as all the lights flicker in the dark. Divali is the prettiest holiday of all!"

Chanda was the first one up in the morning. She shook Morty and Ferdie.

"Wake up! Wake up!" she cried. "I have something to show you."

Morty and Ferdie followed Chanda into the living room.

"Be careful where you step," Chanda's mother said, pointing to the pretty pictures of birds and flowers that decorated the newly whitewashed floor.

"Mother drew these special holiday pictures," Chanda explained. "Now we get to fill them in with colored rice powders."

What fun it was to "paint" the living room floor with colored powders. At the entrance, they filled in one last pattern as a sign of welcome to all who would visit them on Divali.

When they were finished, Chanda's mother sent them to buy pottery oil lamps at the market. The market was bustling with activity. Everyone in the village was shopping for the holiday. Ram was there, too, poking his trunk into places it didn't belong.

"Try to be careful this time," Chanda whispered in his ear.

"Would you mind leading Ram away from my stall?" asked a nervous looking pottery-maker. "This is a bad place for such a clumsy animal!"

Morty and Ferdie hurried off with Chanda to find
some rope to make a leash for Ram. But they were not
fast enough. They got back just in time to hear a terrible
crash.

"Oh no!" cried the potter, as he stared at the piles of
shattered oil lamps at his feet. "Ram has ruined all the
lamps for Divali!"

"How will we light up our village now?" cried Chanda sadly. "Divali will not be the same without pretty lights!" She began to think. It wasn't long before she had an idea.

"Perhaps other villages will have some lanterns to spare," Chanda said. "If we collect a few lanterns from each one, then we will have enough to light up our village!"

"It's worth a try," said Morty.

"It's our only hope," agreed another merchant.

"Maybe we should take Ram with us," Ferdie suggested.

"That's a wonderful idea," replied Chanda. "He's big and strong enough to carry all of us and the lanterns, too!"

While Chanda ran home to ask her parents' permission to make the trip, the village merchants helped Morty and Ferdie get ready to leave.

Someone prepared a basket of food for them.

Someone else filled jugs with water.

Others put a seat on Ram that had big, deep saddle bags, and attached a cart behind the little elephant to hold all the lanterns they hoped to collect.

Chanda returned with good news.

"We can go!" she cried. "We just have to be sure to come home before dark."

She gently tapped three times on Ram's leg with a stick. That was his signal to drop down to his knees so the three friends could climb aboard.

Everyone wished them luck as they started out on their journey. Ram seemed eager to make up for his mistakes. He carried Chanda, Morty, and Ferdie from village to village and knelt down each time so that the neighboring villagers could fill the saddlebags and the cart with as many lanterns as they could spare.

Meanwhile, Mickey arrived at Chanda's house. Her parents told him all about Ram and the broken lanterns.
"I hope they don't get lost," said Mickey.
"Don't worry," said Chanda's mother. "They will be back in time for the celebration."

The sun was just setting as Ram and the three friends
entered the village. Everyone gave a loud cheer when
they saw how many lanterns they had with them.

"Divali is saved!" the villagers cried joyfully.

Mickey helped hang the lanterns while Chanda,
Morty, and Ferdie led Ram away. They still had one more
task to complete.

When the lanterns were lit, everyone came out to admire their beauty and parade through the streets. Leading the villagers was none other than Ram himself.

Chanda and the boys had painted designs and decorations all over Ram. Everyone agreed that Ram made a fine hero.

Morty and Ferdie's eyes shone almost as brightly as the twinkling lights that outlined Chanda's village.

"You were right," they told her. "Divali is the prettiest holiday of all!"

Did You Know…?

There are many different customs and places that make each country special. Do you remember some of the things below from the story?

Southern India is a high, flat plain. It is filled with farmlands and forest, and is separated from the rest of India by mountains.

Two sports played in America originally came from India. *Badminton* is a racket game in which a feathered ball called a *shuttlecock* is hit across a net between two players. *Polo* was first played by Indian horsemen hitting a ball of leaves with long sticks.

Brothers and sisters celebrate
a yearly festival in India.
Each sister ties a bracelet on
her brother's wrist. The brother
promises to protect his sister
and help her whenever she
needs him.

Dancing in India is a popular way to tell stories.
Every movement of the dancer's fingers, hands, and arms
means something special. Through these gestures, the
dancer tells exciting stories of romance and adventure.

Elephants in India work hard. They are trained to carry people, goods, and just about anything else. Some elephants can even carry heavy logs with their trunks. Good job, Ram!

The marketplace is often the busiest place in Indian villages and cities. People come here to buy and sell food, rugs, clothes, toys, and all kinds of things. It's a good place to meet friends, too.

Indian craftspeople are known for the many beautiful things they make by hand, including clothes, pottery, glass, and wood carvings.

Indians often eat a lentil soup called *dal*. It is a popular dish in India and can be black, red, green, or yellow, depending on the kind of lentils used.

Many Indian women wear colorful dresses called *saris*. A sari is a very long piece of cloth that is wrapped around the waist and draped over the shoulders or head.

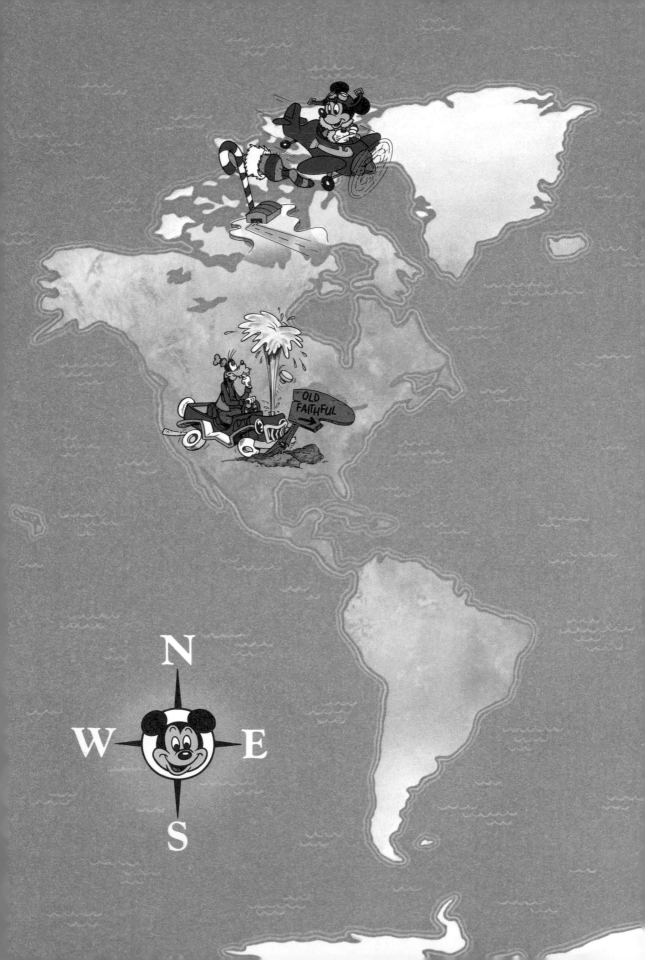